DINOSAUR RESCUE

KYLE MEWBURN & DONOVAN BIXLEY

T-WRECK-ASAURUS

SCHOLASTIC CANADA LTD.

TORONTO NEW YORK LONDON AUCKLAND SYDNEY
MEXICO CITY NEW DELHI HONG KONG BUENOS AIRES

The author would like to point out he doesn't really believe Neanderthals and dinosaurs lived at the same time. He certainly didn't see any dinosaurs when he visited the Stone Age in his time machine while researching this book.

Scholastic Canada Ltd.
604 King Street West, Toronto, Ontario M5V 1E1, Canada

Scholastic Inc.
557 Broadway, New York, NY 10012, USA

Scholastic Australia Pty Limited
PO Box 579, Gosford, NSW 2250, Australia

Scholastic New Zealand Limited
Private Bag 94407, Botany, Manukau 2163, New Zealand

Scholastic Children's Books
Euston House, 24 Eversholt Street, London NW1 1DB, UK

Library and Archives Canada Cataloguing in Publication

Mewburn, Kyle
T-wreck-asaurus / by Kyle Mewburn ; illustrations by Donovan Bixley.
(Dinosaur rescue)
ISBN 978-1-4431-1358-8
I. Bixley, Donovan II. Title. III. Series: Dinosaur rescue

PZ7.M573Tw 2012   j823'.92   C2011-905475-2

6 5 4 3 2 1   Printed in Canada 121   12 13 14 15

Arg's Valley

1. Pterosaur Cliffs
2. Lava Mountain
3. Bog
4. Slimepot Swamp
5. Big Bone Lake
6. Village Fire Pit
7. Arg's Village
8. Stinkooze Pit

Arg's Grandad

Old Drik

Shlok
Arg's best friend

Arg
Caveboy genius

Gurg

Krrk-Krrk
Arg's pet Microceratops

Hng
Arg's big sister

Arg's mother

Arg's father

The many moods of Arg's mother

Happy

Angry

Sad

Confused

Scared

Excited

CHAPTER ONE

When Arg told his mom he was going to Slimepot Swamp to collect brontosaurus poo, she frowned. Arg didn't know if it was a good frown or a bad frown. Sometimes it was hard to tell what his mom was thinking. Stone Age people *always* looked like they were frowning. Even when they weren't. And Arg's mom was frownier than most. Arg's dad said that's why he dragged her into his cave . . .

But that's another story.

"Swamp bad," she grunted. "Dinosaur eat Arg."

Arg grinned. "Don't worry, Mom. I'll be careful. And Krrk-Krrk will protect me. He can smell danger from a hundred spears away."

Krrk-Krrk gave a small microceratops bark.

Krrk-Krrk was a total scaredy-saur.

But he liked going on adventures.

Arg's mom scratched her head and grunted. Most of the time she didn't understand a word Arg said. One time Arg tried to explain that the reason he was a lot smarter than all the other people in his tribe was because his brain was twice as big as everyone else's. Arg didn't know why he'd been born with such a big brain. He just knew it made him smarter. Lots smarter.

But Arg's mom had just scratched her armpits and yawned. It was way too complicated for her little brain to understand. She didn't even know what a brain was. She didn't care, either. She didn't like thinking too much. So Arg gave up. Sometimes it was very lonely being so much cleverer than everyone else.

"Big trouble, Arg scream," his mom said. She lifted him up and squeezed him so hard he thought his head would pop.

Arg tried to squirm loose. But his mom was very strong.

"Arg back before sun go," his mom said. "No come, no din-din. Go hungry."

Arg rolled his eyes. That wasn't a punishment, it was more like a reward! The hunting party was still away. All they'd get to eat tonight would be some rotting berries and moss. A roasted cycad root too, if they were lucky. Arg didn't mind missing that. If he caught something yummy to eat at Slimepot Swamp, he'd make sure he was late.

"Yes, Mom," he said.

His mother grunted but didn't put him down.

Arg's tools

Throwy stones

Multi-purpose Swiss Army rock

Pokey poker

Bonger

She stared at him suspiciously. Then she shoved her finger deep into her nose. When she pulled it out again, there was a big chunk of soft, green snot on the end. She studied it a second before popping it in her mouth.

Arg almost gagged. Sometimes his mom was such a Neanderthal.

As soon as she put him down, Arg ran to his cave.

"Come on, Krrk-Krrk," he said, grabbing his spear and a hollowed storing log. Then off they headed for Slimepot Swamp.

Dinosaur wishbone slingshot

Whacker

Super-fangled whacker

Spear

A small note about clothes

Nobody in Arg's village wears clothes.
But Arg doesn't like walking around naked.
He didn't mind when he was young, but he's nearly eight summers old now.

Arg's wardrobe

**Arg's favourite
sabre-toothed tiger coat**

**Bear foot slippers
for cold nights**

Arg's mom wasn't happy when he started wearing clothes. "You furry. No need more fur," she grunted.

But Arg wasn't as furry as everyone else. "But, Mo-om," Arg moaned. "I'm always cold. And the furs keep me warm. I think clothes are a great idea. Everyone will be wearing them one day."

Arg's mom fished some earwax out of her ear and ate it. "Arg not leave fur lying in cave," she grunted. "Me not brush fur."

Arg's favourite fur is his sabre-toothed tiger coat. Arg ties small fur bags onto his coats. He sticks his hands in them when it's cold. He can put other things in them too. Arg calls the bags "puckets." He doesn't think "puckets" sounds quite right, but he hasn't come up with a better name yet.

Turtle shell helmet for dangerous activities

Puckets good for putting cold hands (and other things) in

Underwear for hot days

Fresh underwear in case of accidents

CHAPTER TWO

Pttthththththththththth!
The sound of brontosaurus toots echoed across the valley. **Pttththththththththththth!**

Brontosauruses had the worst gas in the world. Arg thought it was because they ate only vegetables. Arg didn't like vegetables.

All dinosaurs tooted. A lot! Cave people cut the cheese a lot too. But brontosaurus toots were the hottest, smelliest toots of all. Sometimes Arg worried that all that dinosaur gas would make the world get hotter. He didn't think that would be a good idea because . . .

Well, that's another story too.

Slimepot Swamp was at the end of the valley and was ringed by volcanoes. Rivers of molten lava flowed down all sides. When the lava touched swamp water, it made giant clouds of steam.

GAS DANGER TODAY.

SSS Just plain stinky
ᘓ May cause dizziness
O
X WARNING! Deadly

The steam was so hot, it could cook you in seconds. The swamp bubbled with sulphur and gurgling mud geysers and there were quicksand pits everywhere.

Slimepot Swamp was not a good place to play.

Arg crept along the edge of the swamp collecting brontosaurus poo. If it was still wet, he squashed it into his hollow log. If it was dry, he put it in his puckets.

He kept glancing up. The brontosaurus herd was in the middle of the swamp. Some of them were eating swamp-grass. Some were wallowing in the mud. Brontosauruses weren't dangerous. But they were very clumsy. It wasn't a good idea to get too close.

The swamp was very noisy. The sound of hissing and tooting and brontosaurus roars was deafening. Arg didn't hear the footsteps getting closer. And closer. Then, suddenly…

Screeeeeeeeeeeech!

The T. Rex screech was very loud. And very, VERY close. Arg's ears rang. His heart dropped into his feet. Krrk-Krrk scurried away to hide under a rock. Arg dropped his log and jumped into the swamp. It was his only chance.

He waded towards the brontosauruses. They wouldn't protect him, but the T. Rex might decide to eat one of them instead. Arg hoped the T. Rex was really hungry and didn't just want a tasty cave-kid snack.

The water smelled awful. Almost as bad as Arg's dad after a hunt.

The mud slurped at Arg's feet. He dragged himself forward. His feet got heavier and heavier. It was like walking through his mom's palm-leaf porridge.

Arg got slower and slower. The water rose to his waist. Arg oozed to a stop. The water rose to his chest.

Arg's eyes grew as wide as allosaurus eggs: the water wasn't rising – he was sinking! Quicksand!

Arg knew he was a goner. If the T. Rex didn't eat him, the quicksand would swallow him. Arg couldn't decide what was worse. Then he thought of another possibility: the T. Rex could chomp him in half, and the quicksand could swallow the rest.

Arg groaned. Sometimes he wished he didn't have such a big brain. It was always thinking up stuff like that.

The T. Rex screeched again.

Wait a second, thought Arg. *T. Rexes don't screech like that when they're just about to gobble a cave kid.* (And Arg should know. He'd seen lots of cave kids get gobbled by T. Rexes. He always thought you had to be stupid to get gobbled by a T. Rex. He never imagined he'd get gobbled by a T. Rex too. How embarrassing!)

Arg glanced over his shoulder. His face blushed red.

It wasn't a T. Rex. It was Shlok. Shlok was an expert at making dinosaur calls. Shlok lifted his

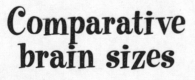

Comparative brain sizes

Average caveman brain

hands to his mouth. He didn't screech again. This time he howled with laughter.

"Arg jump in swamp!" Shlok hooted. "Shlok scare Arg!"

Shlok was Arg's best friend. He wasn't very smart, but he liked playing practical jokes as much as Arg did. Most of the time they did practical jokes together. But sometimes Shlok got jealous because Arg was so much smarter. Then he'd play a practical joke on Arg.

Arg started to smile. Then he remembered the quicksand.

Shlok's brain

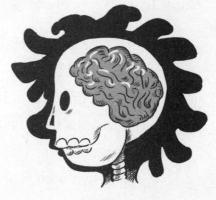

Arg's brain

"Shlok!" he called. "Quick! Get a branch!"

Shlok picked up a stone and threw it at Arg.

"No, a branch!" yelled Arg. The water slurped
over his shoulder.

Shlok grunted and disappeared into the jungle.
A few seconds later, he returned with a very
long branch.

Arg sighed with relief. "Hold it so I can grab it!"

Shlok lifted the branch high above his head…
then threw it. The branch whizzed past Arg's head.

He ducked just in time.

"Don't throw it!" Arg rolled his eyes. "You need to
pull me out!"

Shlok's forehead wrinkled even more than usual.
His jaw jutted forward. It almost hung to his chest.
He was concentrating very hard.

"PULL – ME – OUT!" screamed Arg. He held up his hand. The muddy water gurgled into his ears. Finally, Shlok understood. He found another branch. It was just long enough. Arg grabbed one end and held on tight. Shlok pulled. The mud tugged Arg's bottom half. Shlok tugged Arg's top half. Arg thought he was going to be torn in half. Then...

Pop!

Shlok hauled Arg free and dragged him to safety.

"Thanks, Shlok." Arg grinned with relief. "That was fun."

Shlok grunted and scratched his bum.

Krrk-Krrk crept out from under the rock. Arg bent down to scratch his ear. He frowned. Krrk-Krrk was still trembling with fear. "It's okay, Krrk-Krrk," said Arg. "It was only Shlok."

A loud T. Rex screech sent goosebumps down Arg's furry neck. He shook his head. "You're not going to fool me again, Shlok."

But it wasn't Shlok this time. Shlok was standing upright (well, as upright as he could), listening carefully. The screech came again. It was definitely a T. Rex this time. A big one. And it was coming from their village.

Arg and Shlok looked at each other. They could tell they were thinking exactly the same thing. All the hunters were away. It was up to them to save their village!

Arg and Shlok sprinted toward their village, their spears swinging at their sides. Arg's knees trembled with fear.

Interesting
facts about
brontosaurus poo

Brontosaurus poo is very useful.

Dry brontosaurus poo can be burnt on the fire. It burns very hot.

It can be used as ammunition for slingshots. It is very hard.

You can suck it like candy. It tastes like licorice.

Fresh brontosaurus poo is even more useful.

Arg's dad puts fresh brontosaurus poo on the axles of his hunting wagon. It is very greasy.

Brontosaurus poo can be used like paint. It is gooey and green. Brontosaurus poo green is Arg's favourite colour. Arg paints everything with brontosaurus poo. He paints his cave. He paints his hunting club and his spear. He paints himself with brontosaurus poo too.

Arg's mom doesn't like Arg painting himself with brontosaurus poo. She says it smells disgusting. She prefers swamp mud mixed with pterodactyl egg yolk. Arg's dad uses T. Rex blood. And his older sister, Hng, likes mushed pollen.

Stone Age people paint themselves nearly every day. Nobody knows why. They just do. Arg thinks it's because it's more fun than having a bath.

Stone Age caves smell terrible.

Arg's family cave

CHAPTER THREE

The track to the village was littered with broken branches and snapped tree trunks. It looked like a hurricane had swept through. But hurricanes didn't leave footprints. Especially not very, very big, T. Rex-shaped footprints.

Arg gulped. The T. Rex must be massive. And very angry too.

T. Rexes were predators. They were always stalking through the jungle looking for an easy meal. Lucky for cave people, they weren't very good at creeping. You could hear them coming a mile away. However, they didn't normally go around breaking branches or snapping tree trunks. So something must have annoyed this T. Rex.

Arg and Shlok ran as fast as they could. Krrk-Krrk ran behind, making fearful whining cries. Arg felt like whining too, but he clenched his teeth instead.

He glanced at Shlok. He couldn't tell what his friend was thinking. Knowing Shlok, he probably wasn't thinking anything at all. He was too dumb to be scared.

They felt the ground trembling. They heard
screams and yells. Then a mighty screech shook
the trees.

Arg and Shlok swapped nervous glances. Shlok's
eyes were watery. His black tongue looked like a
snake, crawling over dry lips. He wasn't too dumb
to be scared after all.

They reached the village clearing. It was a
disaster area.

SWAT

Broken branches were lying everywhere. The bonfire pit was trampled. Half-dried animal hides were hanging in trees. The tribe's flint pile was scattered and shattered and stomped into dust.

Arg looked around. He could see old people and babies huddled at the entrances of their caves. They looked scared. Everyone else was doing their best to scare the T. Rex away.

Arg's mom kept charging at the T. Rex, swinging a burning stick. Shlok's mom and grandma were throwing rocks down from their cave. All the cave kids were firing stones with their slingshots.

The T. Rex was crashing and stumbling in circles. Each time it spun around, its tail sent something – or someone – flying.

Arg scratched his head. Something wasn't quite right.

Before he could figure out what it was, Old Drik
shuffled out of her cave. Old Drik was very old. She
was almost blind and completely deaf. She looked
very angry and shuffled straight toward the T. Rex,
wagging her finger.

"Me sleep," she grunted. "Too much bang-bang.
Go away!"

Arg covered his eyes. He couldn't watch.

The T. Rex gave a loud screech. Arg waited to hear the sound of crunching bones. Instead, he heard another screech. Then a loud crash.

Arg peered through his fingers. Old Drik was still wagging her finger. But the T. Rex wasn't listening. It charged a tree and dragged itself along a branch.

The branch snapped off and crashed to the ground.

The T. Rex screeched louder. Then charged the other way. Arg scowled in concentration. It didn't make any sense.

Suddenly, a loud battle call echoed through the clearing. Arg shook his head as Gurg burst out of hiding. Gurg was only two summers older than Arg.

He wasn't strong enough to kill a T. Rex. Not by a long way. But Gurg was too dumb to realise that. He charged the T. Rex, waving his spear.

The T. Rex didn't pay any attention. It scraped its back against the cliff. Rocks and dirt tumbled into the clearing. A cave baby almost toppled down too. Its mother caught it just in time.

A big boulder nearly hit Gurg. He leapt over it and lunged at the T. Rex, but his spearhead wasn't sharp enough to penetrate the dinosaur's tough skin.

Arg rolled his eyes. Gurg was always too lazy to sharpen his spear.

Gurg wasn't giving up. He shuffled back twenty paces. Then, with a bloodcurdling scream, he charged and threw himself at the T. Rex. This time, his spear split open the dinosaur's scaly skin. Blood spurted everywhere.

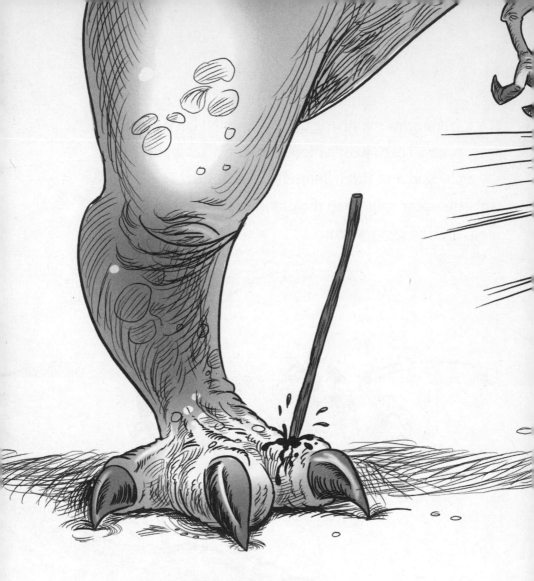

The T. Rex jerked as if it had been stung by a bee.
Its head spun around. It looked very confused.
When it noticed Gurg digging his spear into its foot,

it bent down and . . . **CHOMP!**

It chomped Gurg in half and spat him out.

Arg shrugged. He never liked Gurg anyway.

And there were more important things to think about. Like why the T. Rex didn't eat Gurg. T. Rexes *never* missed a chance for an easy meal.

"Me fight T. Rex," grunted Shlok. "Me die like brave hunter."

You die like stupid cave kid, thought Arg. *Just like Gurg.*

Shlok got ready to charge, but Arg stopped him.

The T. Rex threw its tiny arms in the air and spun around again.

"Wait! I've just figured out what's wrong!"
Arg grinned.

T. Rexes were ruthless killers. They could kill with one bite. But this T. Rex wasn't trying to kill anyone. It wasn't hungry. It was itchy! It was trying to scratch its back, but its arms were too short to reach!

The never-before-told secret of Stone Age hunting

Stone Age men don't go hunting every day. It's too much hard work. They only hunt when they get sick of eating nuts and berries.

Hunting trips can take a long time. Dinosaurs aren't very clever, but they're clever enough to know that Stone Age people want to eat them. So they usually stay far away.

Hunters don't hunt big dinosaurs like brontosauruses or T. Rexes. Hunters say that's because these dinosaurs are too big to carry. But really it's because they are too dangerous. Hunters like to have fun and show off. They don't like to get squashed or eaten.

Sometimes they only *pretend* to go hunting. Instead of heading for the dinosaur grazing places, they go to a secret place. They drink fermented dinosaur milk and tell stories all day.

Sometimes they play a game called Golaf. They hit dinosaur eyeballs along the ground with sticks. The winner is the person who loses the most eyeballs. Golaf is a very stupid game.

While the hunting party is away, the rest of the tribe collects dry wood and piles it up in the bonfire pit. When the hunters return, there is an enormous feast. Everyone eats and eats until they can't eat any more. Sometimes they eat so much they vomit. Then they eat some more.
If it's a very good meal,
they eat their vomit too.

Meat has to be eaten right away. Even Stone Age people don't like eating maggots . . . unless they are roasted. Then they taste like popcorn.

CHAPTER FOUR

Arg had fleas once. They itched and itched. It almost drove him crazy. His mom preened him for hours. She brushed through his light coat, chasing one flea after another. When she caught them, she popped them into her mouth. But there were too many fleas to eat. After a while, she was so full she had to lie down. And Arg was still crawling with fleas.

Arg's mom thought he got the fleas from his sabre-toothed tiger coat. She was always blaming Arg's clothes. But Arg knew exactly where he got them from – his grandad. There were all sorts of creepy-crawly things living on Arg's grandad. That's because he never let anyone preen him.

Arg tried everything to get rid of the fleas. Smoky

fires. Cold baths. He even thought about shaving off all his fur with a sharp flint – that's how desperate he was.

Finally, Arg got the idea to lie in a pool of hot mud. What a relief!

He almost felt sorry for the T. Rex. But how was he going to get it to lie down in a pool of hot mud? T. Rexes didn't like taking orders. Not from anybody. And the nearest hot mud pool was in Slimepot Swamp.

Arg looked around. His tribe were starting to get desperate. They were sure the T. Rex was trying to eat them all. All the moms were huddled behind a rock, sharpening their spears.

Arg knew they were getting ready to charge. If

that happened, the T. Rex might forget its itch and
attack them. Arg's mom was a good spear thrower.
But it would take a hundred spears to kill a T. Rex.
They'd just make it angry. And an angry T. Rex could
kill them all!

"We've got to do something," Arg hissed.
He glanced around at Shlok. His stomach
did a somersault.

Shlok must have had the same idea. He was

creeping along the edge of the clearing – inching
closer to the T. Rex.

There was no time to lose.

Arg sprinted across the clearing, heading straight
for the T. Rex. He hoped he was right about the itch.
If he wasn't . . .

The T. Rex twisted around. It tried to drag its back
against a broken tree stump but lost its balance and

stumbled backwards. It nearly stepped right on Arg.
Arg dodged and weaved. One foot smashed beside
him. The next whistled past his ear.

Suddenly he was right underneath the T. Rex. Its
underbelly was thin and pale. He could see its heart
throbbing just beneath. If he shoved his spear
upwards as hard as he could, he might be able to kill
it. He'd be a hero.

Arg held his spear tightly with both hands and
stared at the throbbing spot. It was an easy target.

The T. Rex didn't know he was there. But he had only a few seconds. If he wanted to do it, he had to do it now.

Slowly, he shook his head. He didn't want to be a hero. And he didn't want to kill the T. Rex. It wasn't smart to kill for no reason. He didn't want the T. Rex to kill any more of his tribe, either. Especially not Shlok or his mom.

Arg's mom burst out from behind her rock. She gave a bloodcurdling scream. Arg's older sister, Hng, didn't move. Arg wasn't sure, but it looked like she was smiling.

Arg sprinted over to the huge tree in the middle of the clearing. The branches were far apart. He needed both hands to climb it, so he dropped his spear and hauled himself up. Higher and higher.

As soon as Arg's mom saw him climbing to safety, she retreated back behind the rock. Hng scowled in disappointment.

Shlok didn't see Arg clambering up the tree. He thought Arg had been squashed by the T. Rex. He gave a mighty growl and charged. Arg yelled, but Shlok couldn't hear a thing above the dinosaur's roar.

Arg stared. He hoped Shlok wasn't as stupid as Gurg. If he tried to spear the T. Rex, he'd be crunched too.

Shlok sprinted closer. The T. Rex swung around. When Shlok was close enough, he launched his spear.

It sailed through the air like a rocket . . .

It whizzed past the T. Rex's ear . . .

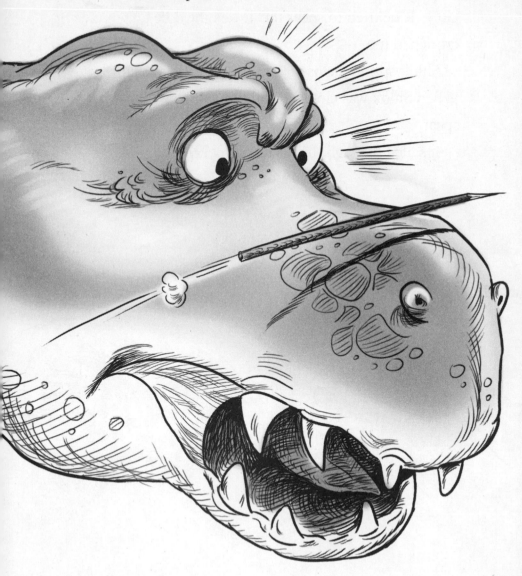

and harpooned into the tree . . .

T'HWACK

right below Arg.

   Arg shook his head. Shlok was
such a terrible shot. How could
anyone miss something as big as
a T. Rex?

   Arg knew it was up to him.
He just had to get to the top of
the tree before Shlok accidentally
speared him.

He tried to climb higher. He couldn't move. The spear had gone right through his sabre-toothed coat. He was stuck! He tried to pull the spear out. But it was buried deep in the trunk. Shlok wasn't a good aim, but he was very strong.

Arg wriggled and squirmed. He couldn't pull his

coat loose. The sabre-toothed tiger skin was very tough.

There was only one thing Arg could do.

He slipped out of his coat and clambered higher.
His face flushed red with embarrassment. He didn't
feel smart. He felt like a stupid, naked monkey.
And everyone was watching him.

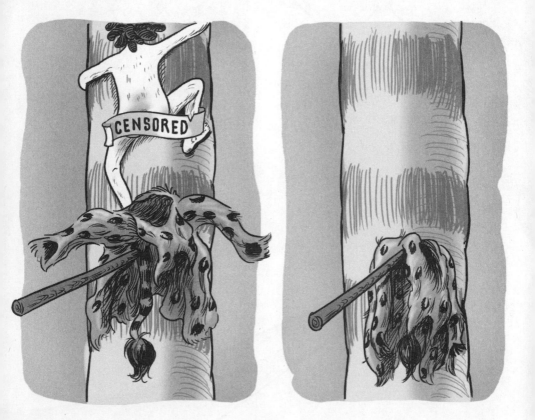

He reached the top
branch, then
squatted, waiting.

The T. Rex danced across
the clearing. It slammed
against the tree.

Arg took a deep breath, then jumped. He landed on the T. Rex's back. It started to buck wildly. Its head whipped around. Razor-sharp teeth slashed past Arg's nose.

Arg held onto its scales with all his strength. Lucky its arms were too short to reach Arg.

The T. Rex's whole back rippled and twitched. Arg's hands curled into claws.

Arg started to scratch as hard as he could.
The T. Rex stumbled backwards. It was heading
straight for the cliff. Arg was going to get crushed!

Arg slipped down the T. Rex's back and scratched
harder. The creases in his forehead filled with sweat.
His furry legs ached with tiredness.

Then the T. Rex gave an ear-shattering screech . . .
and sighed to a halt.

Arg started to sigh with relief. The T. Rex didn't move. It started to make a strange purring sound. The sound vibrated through its whole body,

vibrating Arg too. His teeth chattered. His
body trembled. But he kept scratching.
Suddenly, the vibrations stopped.

scratch
scratch
scratch

The T. Rex jerked up.

Arg glanced up and groaned. His whole tribe was charging toward them. They were waving spears and clubs and burning sticks, and yelling as loudly as they could.

The T. Rex spun one way then the other. Behind it, the cliff rose nearly straight up. A wave of shouting cave people were closing in rapidly on all sides.

It was outnumbered; trapped.

It screeched fiercely, then charged. Arg's mom dove out of the way. Spears rained down all around. The T. Rex broke through. It didn't pause when it reached the edge of the clearing; it crashed through the wall of creepers and moss and disappeared into the jungle.

Arg clung tightly to its back, screaming all the way.

CHAPTER FIVE

The T. Rex didn't sidestep around bushes. It didn't dodge around volcanic boulders. It didn't change course for anything. It crashed through the jungle like a giant unstoppable tank.

THWACK

Branches whipped Arg's face. Vines swung down and tried to strangle him. But he held on.

T. Rexes could run very fast. Everything whizzed past. Arg couldn't tell which way they were going. If the T. Rex ran too far, Arg would never find his way back to the clearing. He'd be left all alone in a dark, scary jungle full of boy-eating dinosaurs.

Lost forever . . . or at least until he got eaten. No dinosaur would care how big Arg's brain was.

They plunged out of the jungle into a small, swampy clearing. A tall cliff blocked their way. Arg looked up . . . and up . . . and up. He couldn't see the top. It disappeared into the sky. The T. Rex didn't turn. It didn't slow down. It ran as fast as it could. It splashed through the swamp – heading straight for the cliff.

They were going to crash!

Arg closed his eyes.
He couldn't watch.
This was going to hurt.
   He counted silently
on his fingers.
         One . . .

               two . . .

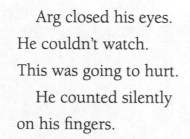

The sound of the jungle faded. The only things Arg could hear were the T. Rex's heavy breathing and his own pounding heart. Everything was echoing. That was strange.

Arg slowly opened one eye . . .

The other eye sprang open too.

He blinked both eyes. They were definitely open but he couldn't see a thing! Was he blind from fright? No . . . he could see a faint light ahead. It was getting brighter. They must be in a tunnel.

Suddenly they burst into light. The T. Rex slowed
to a standstill and stood, puffing heavily.

Arg looked around. There was no jungle on this
side of the tunnel. No swamps or bubbling geysers,

either. There were rolling green fields dotted with
wildflowers as far as he could see. It wasn't at all
scary like the jungle. It looked kind of friendly even.

The fields were full of dinosaurs too. Dinosaurs of

every kind. They weren't screeching and roaring
at each other. They were hardly even passing gas.
They were grazing peacefully, side by side.
The valley was so peaceful, Arg could hear

CENSORED

a river chuckling over rocks.

A raptor lumbered toward them.

That meant trouble!

Arg leapt
off the T.
Rex's back into
the branches of
a nearby tree.

Bad move. The raptor
spotted Arg and stomped
towards him.

The T. Rex lumbered to
block, then screeched loudly
and bared its fangs. The raptor scurried away.

Arg scrambled higher as the T. Rex leaned closer. Arg smelt its bad breath. Its teeth gleamed in its very big mouth.

"You can't eat me!" gulped Arg. His mouth felt like it was full of fur. "I helped you!"

The T. Rex blinked. "What did you just say?"

Arg's mouth gaped open. Did the T. Rex just speak?

"I was saying it wouldn't be fair to eat me," he said.

"You can talk!" said the T. Rex.

"Of course I can talk," grumbled Arg. "I'm not stupid."

"No, indeed," chuckled the T. Rex as he studied Arg from every angle. "Hmmmm. Has your brain *always* been that big?"

"No, I found it under a cycad," said Arg, rolling his eyes. "DUH!"

The T. Rex almost blushed. "Sorry. Stupid question, I know. I guess I'm not really used to talking to other clever creatures."

"Can all dinosaurs talk?" asked Arg.

The T. Rex laughed. "No. Lucky for me! I'd feel terrible eating prey that was saying 'please don't eat me.'" The T. Rex laughed until he stopped.

"Sorry about your friend, by the way," the T. Rex said. He grimaced with embarrassment. "I didn't mean to chomp him. But he was just *so* annoying. Poking my foot with his spear like that. It really hurt."

Arg shrugged. "That's all right. He's not my friend anyway."

Arg had a million questions but there wasn't time for a single one.

The T. Rex sprang to attention. "Oh dear, I better get you back home before someone tracks you here. Quick, jump on my back!"

The T. Rex dropped Arg in the jungle beside the clearing. Arg could hear his mom performing a death wail. She was very upset. She thought he must be dead.

The T. Rex started to leave.

"What's your name?" asked Arg.

The T. Rex frowned. "My name?"

"You know. What your family and your friends call you," said Arg.

"I don't have any family. Or friends," sighed the T. Rex.

"My name's Arg." Arg held out his hand.

The T. Rex shook it. "I think I'll call you Skeet . . . if you don't mind."

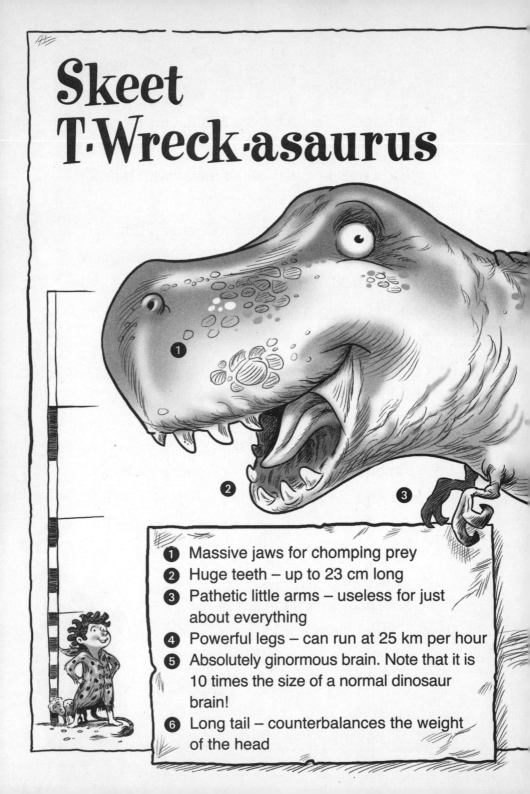

Skeet T·Wreck·asaurus

1. Massive jaws for chomping prey
2. Huge teeth – up to 23 cm long
3. Pathetic little arms – useless for just about everything
4. Powerful legs – can run at 25 km per hour
5. Absolutely ginormous brain. Note that it is 10 times the size of a normal dinosaur brain!
6. Long tail – counterbalances the weight of the head

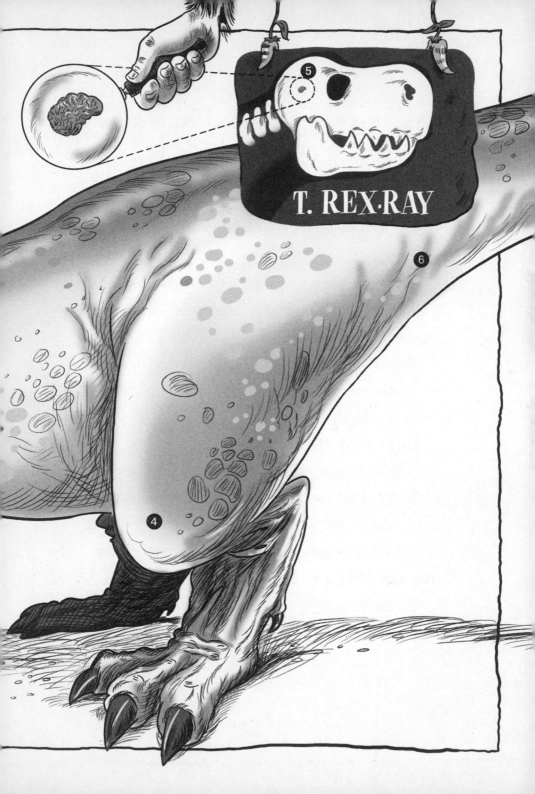

T. REX·RAY

The T. Rex thought about that. Then he smiled. "No, Arg, I don't mind at all."

"What were you doing in our valley, Skeet?" Arg suddenly asked. If Arg lived in a friendly valley like Skeet's, he'd never set foot outside. It was way too dangerous.

Skeet gave Arg a long, sad look. Then he sighed. It was a very long sigh. Very smelly too. Arg held his breath and waited.

"When I was growing up, there used to be dinosaurs everywhere. But every year there are fewer and fewer."

Arg nodded. "That's what my dad says."

Skeet sighed again. "When I found the secret valley, I knew I had to try and rescue as many of us as I could. Before we all become extinct. But it's very hard work. Dangerous too. Dinosaurs can be very stubborn. And stupid."

"So can humans," said Arg. He started sighing too. But stopped halfway as another brilliant idea exploded in his huge brain. "Maybe I could help!"

Skeet chuckled. "What a great idea!" He gave Arg a big wink. "Us clever creatures should stick together, eh? See you later, Arg."

Arg's smile was wide as a half moon as he pushed through the last curtain of creepers. He might be the only human with a big brain but somehow he didn't feel so lonely any more.

He sprinted across the clearing, hooting and hollering all the way.